7

GET READY . . . GET SET . . . READ!

BAT'S SURPRISE

by
Foster & Erickson

Illustrations by
Kerri Gifford

BARRON'S

"How can I make something o
my own?" said Bat.

"I need help.
I must get help."

"Hello, Pug. Hello, bugs.
Can you help me?"

"No," said Pug.
"You must make something of
your own."

The bug club ran to the old red rug to make something.

And Bat sat.

"Hello, Lop. Hello, Pop.
Can you help me?"

"No," said Pop and Lop.
"We must make something of
our own."

Pop and Lop went to the
shop to make something.

And Bat sat and sat.

"Hello, Ned, Ted, and Jed.
Can you help me?"

"No, Bat," they said.
"You must make something of
your own."

Ned, Ted, and Jed ran to the shed to make something.

And Bat sat and sat and sat.

Yes, all day long Bat sat.
Trish, Pat, Ed, and Rat all
saw Bat.

They would not help him.
They all ran to make
something of their own.

Swish, slop, trim, chug,
drop, plop, splat, tug.

Day in and day out
Bat sat.

"Hello, Bat. The day is here.
Come see what
we have made."

"Yes," said Bat.
"Let's see what *we*
all have made."

Lop, Pop . . .

Nat, Ned . . .

In the Jug
by Pug and the Bugs

My Wish
by TRiSH the fish

Pug, Trish . . .

The Hat Shop
by *Pat* the Cat

Hugs.
by ED

Pat, Ed . . .

All About Me
by
the fat Rat

Swim, swim!

by Jed

the fat Rat, Jed, Ted . . .

Upon the Rim
by TED

Something Funny!
by Slim Jim

Slim Jim and what?
Surprise!
Bat made something . . .

"Bat, how did you make
something of your own?"

"We saw you sit
day in and day out."

"I had help from all of you."

DEAR PARENTS AND EDUCATORS:

Welcome to **Get Ready...Get Set...Read!**

We've created these books to introduce children to the magic of reading.

Each story in the series is built around one or two word families. For example, *A Mop for Pop* uses the OP word family. Letters and letter blends are added to OP to form words such as TOP, LOP, and STOP.

This **Bring-It-All-Together** book serves as a reading review. When your children have finished *Find Nat, The Sled Surprise, Sometimes I Wish, A Mop for Pop,* and *The Bug Club,* it is time to have them read this book. *Bat's Surprise* uses the characters and words introduced in the first five **Get Ready . . . Get Set . . . Read!** stories. (Each set in the series will be followed by two review books.)

Bring-It-All-Together books provide:
•much needed vocabulary repetition for developing fluency.
•longer stories for increasing reading attention spans.
•new stories with familiar characters for motivating young readers.

We have created these **Bring-It-All-Together** books to help develop confidence and competence in your young reader. We wish you much success in your reading adventures.

Kelli C. Foster, Ph.D.
Educational Psychologist

Gina Clegg Erickson, MA
Reading Specialist

All inquiries should be addressed to:
Barron's Educational Series, Inc.
250 Wireless Boulevard
Hauppauge, New York 11788

International Standard Book No. 0-8120-1735-8
Library of Congress Catalog Card No.

Library of Congress Cataloging-in-Publication Data

Available upon request.

PRINTED IN HONG KONG
19 18 17 16 15

Titles in the

Series:

SET 1

Find Nat
The Sled Surprise
Sometimes I Wish
A Mop for Pop
The Bug Club
BRING-IT-ALL-TOGETHER BOOKS
What a Day for Flying!
Bat's Surprise

SET 2

The Tan Can
The Best Pets Yet
Pip and Kip
Frog Knows Best
Bub and Chub
BRING-IT-ALL-TOGETHER BOOKS
Where Is the Treasure?
What a Trip!

SET 3

Jake and the Snake
Jeepers Creepers
Two Fine Swine
What Rose Does Not Know
Pink and Blue
BRING-IT-ALL-TOGETHER BOOKS
The Pancake Day
Hide and Seek

SET 4

Whiptail of Blackshale Trail
Colleen and the Bean
Dwight and the Trilobite
The Old Man at the Moat
By the Light of the Moon
BRING-IT-ALL-TOGETHER BOOKS
Night Light
The Crossing

SET 5

Tall and Small
Bounder's Sound
How to Catch a Butterfly
Ludlow Grows Up
Matthew's Brew
BRING-IT-ALL-TOGETHER BOOKS
Snow in July
Let's Play Ball